Always By My Side

By
Susan Kerner

Illustrated by
Ian P. Benfold Haywood

STAR BRIGHT BOOKS
Cambridge, Massachusetts

Published in the United States of America by Star Bright Books, Inc.

The name Star Bright Books and the Star Bright Books logo are registered
trademarks of Star Bright Books, Inc. Please visit: www.starbrightbooks.com.
For bulk orders, email: orders@starbrightbooks.com, or call customer service
at: (617) 354-1300.

Hardback ISBN-13: 978-1-59572-336-9
Star Bright Books / MA / 00103130
Printed in China / Toppan / 10 9 8 7 6 5 4 3 2 1

Paperback ISBN-13: 978-1-59572-337-6
Star Bright Books / MA / 00103130
Printed in China / Toppan / 10 9 8 7 6 5 4 3 2 1

Library of Congress Cataloging-in-Publication Data

Kerner, Susan.
 Always by my side / by Susan Kerner ; illustrations by Ian P. Benfold Haywood.
    p. cm.
 Summary: "A rhyming story written to help children understand that a dad's love
is forever. Even if they grow up without his presence in their lives"-- Provided by
publisher.
 ISBN 978-1-59572-336-9 (hardcover) -- ISBN 978-1-59572-337-6 (pbk.)
 [1. Stories in rhyme. 2. Fathers--Fiction. 3. Loss (Psychology)--Fiction.] I. Benfold
Haywood, Ian P., ill. II. Title.
 PZ8.3.K3985Al 2013
 [E]--dc23
                              2012019398

For Lily Alan, our living dream.
For William.
For Nikhil, Abi, and Amelia.
Blessings all around us.

If you ask me where my daddy is,
  this is what I'll say:
He's in me and around me,
  never far away.

He's in the trees with their shimmering leaves,

and in the lapping waves.

He's in the wind that blows the sails,

and in the sunshine's rays.

And when I hear the birds in song,
or barking dogs at play,
I know that he is speaking to me
in a very special way. . . .

He's saying, "My pumpkin, my little one,
  it's a wonder to watch you grow.

I'm shadowing you from all around,

oh, how I love you so!"

So if I trip on a stepping-stone,

or get scraped when climbing trees,

I know the hurt will go away,
he's watching over me.

My daddy is in the air I breathe,
in the leaves that land in my hair . . .

In the blades of grass that tickle my feet,

in the curious nature we share.

And when I hum to myself, or sing out loud,

or move my hands in a certain way,

Mama kisses my cheek and smiles at me,
  "You're a lot like daddy," she'll say.

"He's in your eyes, you've got his nose,
  and your heart is as large as his.
You're your own little soul, sweet precious child,
  but proudly I'll tell you this:

No matter the day, the month, the year,
   the weather, the tears, or smiles . . .
Daddy is always by your side,
   guiding you all the while."

"So as you brighten the world with your sparkling life,
with an all-knowing smile you'll say,
'My daddy is in me and everywhere . . .
he's just here in a different way.'"